MAS
MINIATURES

MASTER OF MINIATURES

Jim Shepard

SOLID OBJECTS

NEW YORK

Printed in Canada

Design by Erik Rieselbach

ISBN-13: 978-0-9844142-3-9
ISBN-10: 0-9844142-3-1

Library of Congress Control Number: 2010933948

SOLID OBJECTS
P.O. Box 296
New York, NY 10113

MASTER OF MINIATURES

Once again he weathered an afternoon of unease and little progress. He'd forgotten that today was the Star Festival, one of his wife's favorites, and was beginning to wonder at which he was more adept: hurting Masano inadvertently or intentionally. He'd settled into the back seat that morning and spread onto his lap his section of the production board, glued on heavy stock and color-coded, when the driver reminded him about the festival. The driver had noticed the paper cows and kimonos Masano had hung in their potted bamboo out front. They had to have been there when Tsuburaya came home the night before.

The driver at that point had already turned onto the main street and Tsuburaya considered asking to be returned to his home, but then finally said, "Oh, keep going." Immediately he'd understood how that compounded his offense. He imagined himself telling Masano, "I forgot. And when I remembered, I kept going anyway."

She had signed the first love note she'd ever sent to him Shokujo, the name of the Weaver Princess Star, the central figure of the Festival. It had been a reference to the extent to which their discipline for work had suffered in the face of their feelings. According to the legend, the princess had fallen in love with a cowherder; the king had allowed them to marry as a reward for their diligence and industry, but their lovemaking had become for them such a delirium that she had neglected her weaving, and the herder had allowed his cows to stray, so in his exasperation the king had forced them to remain on opposite sides of the Milky Way, to approach each other only once a year. Every July Masano had celebrated the Festival, in recent years more and more often with only Akira, their youngest child. The previous July, while Tsuburaya had looked on, she had shown Akira through his toy telescope how on this night and this night alone the Weaver Princess Star and the Herdboy Star were allowed to meet on the banks of the river of heaven. Tsuburaya had watched as if she were having this conversation with her son in order to have it with him. And if it rained? Akira had asked. If it rained, his mother told him, the two stars had to wait an additional year.

He was falling behind everywhere: in his wife's affections and his work's responsibilities. But in the case of the latter, whether he put in fourteen- or sixteen-hour days, each evening left his production team with still more to accomplish, with principal photography set to commence one way or the other on August 1st.

He told his staff whenever they protested that there was no sense in blaming Tanaka, since he hadn't misled anyone. "Well, then he's the first producer who hasn't," one of his assistants grumbled. But it was true, Tsuburaya reminded them: at the meeting at which Tsuburaya had agreed to come aboard, Tanaka had begun by saying, "The good news is: do you want to make this movie with me, or not? The bad news is, we won't have enough time."

Tanaka had a huge hit with *Eagles of the Pacific* a year earlier, in 1953, but only bad luck since. Two projects collapsed when rights he'd thought were in hand turned out to be too expensive, and the most recent production had been all set to go until the Indonesian government panicked in the face of all the anti-Japanese protests and cancelled the cast and crew's visas. Tanaka said he spent the flight back from Jakarta bathed in his own sweat. Just as Toho was poised to regain its market leadership, its hottest young producer had allowed its biggest project of the year to blow up in his face. He'd telephoned from the Jakarta airport to ask Mori, the executive production manager, how soon he'd need to come up with a replacement for that spot in the production slate, and Mori had answered that he'd better have one by the time he landed. He spent the flight peering miserably out his window at the endless ocean and found his mind wandering to *Lucky Dragon No. 5*. He claimed he'd been so animated when his big idea hit him that the woman beside him had been startled out of her sleep.

In March the Americans had detonated a fifteen megaton hydrogen weapon over Bikini Atoll in the Central Pacific, and *Lucky Dragon No. 5* was one of those little trawlers out for tuna that found itself inside the test zone. They'd been where they were supposed to be but the detonation was twice as large as predicted. They reported seeing the sun rise in the west and then being covered by a powdery white ash for the hour that it took them to retrieve their nets. Back in port it was determined that all twenty-three crew members and their entire haul had been heavily contaminated. And it turned out that the radioactive tuna from other trawlers had entered the Japanese market before the contamination was discovered, and the result was months of nuclear fear and anti-American hostility. Tabloids had called it the Americans' third atomic attack on Japan.

The year before, Tsuburaya had forced Tanaka to go to see his beloved *King Kong*, which had just earned four times as much in its worldwide re-release as it had originally, and Tanaka had also been impressed by the global numbers for Warner Brothers' *The Beast from 20,000 Fathoms,* the story of a dinosaur thawed from its hibernation

6

by American nuclear testing in Baffin Bay.

The United States government estimated that 856 ships in the Japanese fishing fleet had been exposed to radiation, and that more than five hundred tons of fish had to be destroyed, and offered a settlement for the survivors that the Japanese government declined to accept. Tanaka recounted that it struck him as he looked out over the Pacific below that the stories could be combined; and for the rest of the flight he scribbled on the back of a folder that his seatmate had lent him the outline of a story in which a prehistoric creature was awakened by an H-bomb test in the Pacific and then went on to destroy Tokyo.

When Tsuburaya finally returned home for dinner on the night of the Star Festival, Masano served soba noodles and mashed fish. While he ate, she was sober and quiet. He mentioned again by way of conversation a cough that wouldn't go away and she prepared for him without comment what she called her broth of the seven plants, which included shepherd's purse, chickweed, parsley, cottonweed, and radish. She sat with him while he drank it and, once he finished, told him he should smoke less.

For months his project was known at Toho only as Project G, for giant, but lately the staff had taken to calling it *Gojira*, a fusion of the word for gorilla and the one for whale, because of the monster's agility and size. Tanaka and Honda, the director, liked that as much as anything else anyone had come up with.

Upon leaving the following morning Tsuburaya noticed the telescope in the entryway and remembered to ask how the star-viewing had gone. Masano asked how he thought it could have gone, given that it had rained.

The rest of the morning was spent laboring through an interview with the *Weekly Asahi*. The reporter, a young man with goggle-sized glasses, seemed to prize his own skepticism and asked each of his questions as if jabbing a tied dog with a stick. Did Eiji Tsuburaya, the Master of Miniatures and head of Toho's Special Arts Department, feel the burden of his responsibility for the visual effects on which Toho's new flagship production would either float or sink? Tsuburaya assured him that he did. Was it true there was a nuclear subtext to the story? Tsuburaya admitted that there was. And would Mr. Tsuburaya be willing to favor the *Weekly Asahi*'s readers with an exclusive first glimpse of the movie's monster? Mr. Tsuburaya would not.

Eiji Tsuburaya was born in the village of Sukagawa, two hundred and twenty kilometers north of Tokyo in the Fukushima prefecture, and his grandmother and uncle told him every day of his childhood that he'd been delivered on a date propitious for creativity. His parents were Nichiren

Sect Buddhists and as members of the rural gentry had been granted exclusive license to operate the local general goods store, which remained the main clearinghouse, in that region, for sake, soy, and miso. His mother died when she was nineteen and he was three. In both of the photographs of her which remained, she appeared birdlike and consumptive and tilted him toward the camera much as a schoolgirl might display an examination on which had been scrawled a failing grade. In both she seemed to regard the photographer with a kind of pensive anxiety.

With his father subsequently forever at the store, he was raised by his grandmother Natsu and his uncle Ichiro. He and Ichiro were so close in age that his uncle seemed more like an older brother, and so people stopped using Tsuburaya's given name, which meant first son, and started calling him Eiji, or second son.

When he was nine Ichiro took him to see Tokugawa and Hino at the Yoyogi Parade Grounds. Captains in the Imperial Army, they were aviation pioneers who'd made the first successful powered flights in Japan. He spent the next four years teaching himself how to build model airplanes out of wood, especially Tokugawa's Henry Farman biplane. He'd wake each morning at four and light his lamp and work until he had to leave for school and then, when classes were dismissed, he'd rush home and pick up where he'd left off. Once he'd achieved the verisimilitude he sought, he began increasing the scale until he was working on aircraft so large

9

their wingspans no longer fit into his room. His father disapproved, but Tsuburaya believed he was building something that would fly him away and around the world. The bigger models ended up causing enough of a stir with the neighbors that the local newspaper did a feature about him entitled "The Child Craftsman." And throughout his career Tsuburaya was teased about the fact that the first time he saw a motion picture, he found himself more fascinated with the projector than with what was going on onscreen.

Akira was their third child and second son, born much later than the other two children. Their daughter, Miyako, had died in her sleep two years after her birth. She'd had a small fever and called out in the night to Masano, who told her that she would be fine and then fell back asleep after everything had quieted.

For three months afterwards Masano could not be induced to leave the house. Neither her family nor her friends had any effect. She came around only mechanically at first to the notion that they still had a son to raise, and Hajime, who was two years older than Miyako, cried himself to sleep each night in terror and helplessness while his mother gently stroked his head.

Tsuburaya was then a camera operator and kept himself busy with his production schedule and with brainstorming apparatuses that would improve his work. He'd patented and sold the Auto Snap, a pedal-operated shutter cable that freed the hands for other tasks, and had also experimented so successfully with smoke pots for in-camera effects that he'd become known around the industry as Smoke Tsuburaya. When he came home, though, such news had to be left at the front door.

Hajime had finally regained his mother's attention by telling her he was collecting stones for the roadside Jizo image. According to the legend, the souls of all dead children went to the underground river where a she-devil got them to pile stones on the bank by assuring them that if they made their piles high enough they could climb to paradise, but then she perpetually knocked over their work. Jizo, a roadside deity, comforted them, and every stone placed in the lap of one of his statues was supposed to have shortened their task. Each morning before school, then, Hajime and Masano would add one or two stones to the nearest statue's pile.

In this way, his wife had pulled herself along, moment by moment. She enjoyed it if her husband sat quietly beside her. She submitted to his ministrations but declined to touch him. She seemed to appreciate being put to bed at night.

That was the year *King Kong* came to Japan. Tsuburaya had seen *The Lost World* some years earlier, but this was staggering: Willis O'Brien had with his little figures and suitcase jungles transformed RKO Radio Pictures from whatever it had been before into a world power. Tsuburaya wrote him with questions but never discovered if his letters had gotten through. He saw the film six times. He took Hajime, who was so terrified that they had to leave in the middle. Without a response from O'Brien, his only recourse was to use his connections to obtain a 35 mm print and break down its effects himself, frame by frame. One evening he brought Masano in from where she was sitting and situated her next to him beside the projector. The following evening he let her remain where she was.

A week after the Star Festival, Tsuburaya was beginning dinner at his desk when Honda telephoned with news of yet another logistical catastrophe, then caught himself in the middle of his narrative and said, "Oh, but today you have to be home. It's the O-Bon." And he was right: of all the days of the year, this was not the one to come home late. If the Star Festival for Masano was all about how exhilarated they'd once been as lovers, the O-Bon was the principal commemoration of her lost little girl. She had reminded Tsuburaya once, at the beginning of the week, and then had not mentioned it again. She'd be celebrating for the full three days, and on the first night she intended that as a family they would light the paper lantern and hang it on the grave to invite their daughter's spirit to come forth and visit their home. On the table for the dead her daughter's meal would already be set out, with tiny portions featuring her favorite dishes. Akira, as always, had been given charge of arranging the display.

Hajime, now nineteen, was invited, but had yet to indicate whether he would appear. Masano had requested his presence when they'd last seen him, on a school holiday, and he'd answered that he'd see what he could do. He then pointed out that he'd finished his technical training, and asked his father whether he might work with him as assistant camera operator on the miniatures team.

Tsuburaya discussed what that would involve, and Masano interrupted to ask if they could return to the subject of their daughter and Hajime's sister. Then Hajime said he would make every effort to join them, and his mother told him he should see that he did.

That night she informed Tsuburaya that she considered their son's request a bad idea, at least for the time being; that he should stay in school; that he didn't need additional training in how to ignore his family. Tsuburaya felt the need to defend his profession.

"Well, at least promise you'll do nothing without consulting me," she finally requested.

"Who Toho hires is none of your concern," he reminded her.

"What you do with our son is my concern," she answered. And neither of them pursued the matter after that.

When Mori and Honda first approached him, he'd been thrilled at the prospect after all of those years of finally being able to work on the kind of stop-motion effects he had so admired in *King Kong*. But when Mori asked him to write up a projected preproduction and shooting schedule for his unit, even after every shortcut he could conceive, he was forced to report that to do the job right he would need a little less than seven years. On the phone he could hear Mori repeating what he'd said to the others in his office, and there was a general hilarity in the background. When Mori returned to the line he was still chuckling. He said he could give Tsuburaya two months for preproduction and another two for shooting.

That left Tsuburaya's department with few options other than what they knew best: miniature building. Which was what everyone expected of him anyway.

His big break had come when Toho was urged by the government during the war to pour nearly all of its resources into *The War at Sea*, the epic charged with the task of persuading the public that the new war with the Americans was one the Japanese could win. Using photographs supplied by the Navy, his unit had recreated Pearl Harbor on a six-acre outdoor set on Toho's backlot, and had done so with such persuasive detail that the footage of the attack on Battleship Row was confiscated by U.S. occupation officials after the war because they'd taken it to be real. The movie returned the highest grosses ever recorded in Japan, tripled his budgets and staff, and ensured that anyone in the country with a special effects problem would seek out the celebrated Tsuburaya.

So if on this new project O'Brien's solutions were denied

to them, it meant only that they had to approach the situation in a new way. This didn't dishearten them, since they already understood that whenever fixed rules were applied to a problem, only parts of the problem might be perceived. They operated on the principle that you weren't ready for a task until you admitted it was beyond you.

He came up with the idea of an entire 1/25 scale miniature set of the capital, detailed inside as well as out in order to be convincing when trampled. Breakaway walls would reveal entire floors with all of their furnishings when the monster sheared away the outside surfaces. Various aspects of the city's infrastructure such as mailboxes or streetlamps would be rendered in wax and melted by huge offscreen heat lamps to simulate the monster's radioactive breath. Small and precisely calibrated pyrotechnic charges would be installed to reproduce the explosive destruction as fuel and automobile gas tanks ignited.

And 1/25 scale would allow a monster of the proper size to be generated by simply putting a man in a suit.

The simplicity of the plan held enormous appeal. He'd always been drawn to the handmade approach, and of course the studio appreciated the relative lack of expense. Something made from nothing was how he liked to put it.

Mori and Honda loved the budget and feared the plan. A man in a suit? Tsuburaya only shrugged at their unease. They either trusted him or they didn't. Proof was stronger than argument.

The day after the logistical catastrophe, Honda called to report that he'd handled it without Tsuburaya's help. Honda was probably Tsuburaya's closest friend, though at that suggestion Masano once responded that she would love to see Honda's face when someone told him as much. Honda was forever sporting an American's rumpled little fishing hat and was fond of walking great distances. He and Tanaka met when hiking the Diamond Mountains in Korea in the early thirties. Mori and Tanaka had both thought Honda would be the perfect director for this new project since he'd had so little trouble with all the visual effects in *Eagles of the Pacific* and had worked so well with Tsuburaya. Having been a longtime assistant to Kurosawa, he had experience dealing with lunatic perfectionists. "Or, in other words, Tsuburaya," Mori had said at their first full staff meeting.

Mori and Tanaka also liked that Honda had no patience for storylines that dawdled. They'd handed a first attempt at the script to the mystery writer Kayama and what he'd produced was far too tame, involving a nondescript dolphin-like creature that attacked only fishing boats and only to feed its insatiable hunger. Most of the story had involved the poor thing swimming this way and that in search of food.

Honda had clearcut Kayama's script, demanding something terrible enough to evoke both the fire raids on Tokyo and the bombings of Hiroshima and Nagasaki. He'd served three tours of duty as an infantryman, been a prisoner of war in China, been repatriated near Hiroshima, and then had wandered the devastation three months after the surrender.

He thought much like Tsuburaya did: that the director, like a department head, had to include in his leadership the responsibility to protect the artisans under his umbrella. And, of course, the responsibility to recruit those artisans. And where were they to be found? They had to have the right sensibility toward beauty; sufficient technical training and scientific knowledge; and a strong will, passion, and creative talent.

Honda claimed he drew his belief in himself from the soil of his life experience. His mother had also died when he was small, and his father soon afterward. He'd been left unable to attend school and had taught himself to read while carrying firewood for his neighbors. He knew that encountering the unfamiliar might involve many errors before a solution was found, and he had an intuition that seemed to draw on an extraordinary visual resourcefulness. When he loved something, he'd exclaim, "Oh, this is spring water!" Again like Tsuburaya, he knew that the craftsman worked with and for his world, but ultimately went his own way, not seeking praise. When *Eagles of the Pacific* premiered, Honda was on a little lake, fishing. Because the objects themselves were one's best signature.

•

As a young man, Tsuburaya had been struck by how different the Japanese hand was from the big, untrained hands of the other races. Masano had a calligrapher's hands, long-fingered and tapering, and he'd been seduced by their dexterity and sensitivity when watching her set out her simple gifts for him in the hospital. The daughter of a Kyoto engineering magnate, she was fond of movie stars and, thanks to her father's influence, was touring the studio when the camera crane Tsuburaya had invented collapsed and he crashed to the floor in front of her. The shattered lens shield had slightly cut her forehead but even so she cradled his face and neck while his assistants came running. She later claimed he'd reached up to touch her injury, but he had no memory of that. On the same afternoon she'd appeared in his hospital room, bearing her gifts, and remaining behind after everyone else had left. They'd married a year later, when she was nineteen.

Their courtship had mostly taken the form of long distance love notes, in which Tsuburaya found a courage of expression based on longing and the safety of isolation. All of us, he wrote later: when we make a little progress, we're captivated by our cleverness.

Their feelings were an act of faith, just as the sublimity of an artisan's pot was a gift and not a calculation. They gave themselves over to those feelings the way lips kissed the thickness of a tea bowl's rim.

They honeymooned in the old Okinawa, which was now gone. Its capital had been a dream city, its narrow streets mossy and hushed, over which dark leaves threw down their shade. Eaves on the ancient red-tiled roofs featured heraldic animals fired from clay.

But lately it seemed to him that their minds were bound by obsessions that deprived them of freedom. They each put in longer days, he in his innovations and his wife in her grieving. All the rituals that had solidified their happiness now reflected back the opposite. In Masano's photo albums of her loss, baby girls on their thirty-third day were taken to the shrine in thanksgiving by their grandmothers, who prayed for their welfare. As always, the tinier the tot, the more brilliantly it was dressed. Some photographs of these celebrations were prominently displayed on the family altar. Or, in the event of the child's death, on the grave.

Tsuburaya's experience was that one who was gone was forgotten, day by day. As his grandmother put it, Destiny's in heaven, and rice dumplings are on the shelf.

But Masano knew spilt water never returned to the tray. And if she forgot, she said, Tsuburaya reminded her by going on with his life. She said that in the face of her unhappiness, he was like a blind man peeping through a fence.

"I'm sorry for my myopia," he told her after the O-Bon had concluded, and after she'd followed some late-night tenderness with despair. He once again had come home nearly at dawn and she'd risen to meet him, backing him across the room with her beautiful hands.

"I suppose it's like that old saying that the lighthouse doesn't shine on its own base," she'd remarked some hours later, while each still smelled of the other's touch.

Before getting fired, Kayama suggested that the comic book artist Abe should design the creature. Abe had been the illustrator for *Kenya Boy*, a series about an orphaned Japanese boy who was lost in Africa and continually had to fight off prehistoric monsters. Why Africa was overrun with prehistoric monsters was never explained. Abe produced a month's worth of designs, each of which was less useful than the previous one. He was finally let go when he put forward a proposal that featured a giant frog's body and a head shaped like a mushroom cloud. With no time to hire another designer, Honda and Tsuburaya decided to simply hybridize a dinosaur of their own conception. Various illustrations were pulled from libraries and children's books and mixed and matched on the drafting table. Of course it would have a Tyrannosaur's head, but an Iguanodon's body seemed an easier fit for a stuntman's requirements, in terms of operating the suit. And Honda added a Stegosaur's back plates along the spine to ensure their creature would appear distinct from any recorded species.

During the clay rendering stage they had his staff experiment with scaly, warty, and alligator skin before settling on the latter. And with that decided, one whole unit was turned over to the suit's construction.

The first version was framed in cloth-covered wire, over which rubber that had been melted in a steel drum was applied in layers. The result was immobile and weighed three hundred and fifty-five pounds. In the next attempt, the cloth itself was painted with the base coat, so only two layers of rubber were necessary, but the result was still a staggeringly heavy two hundred and twenty pounds. But after a month of further futility, they had to concede that rubber applied any less thickly would crack at the joints, so the second version would have to do.

To minimize the length of time the poor stuntman would have to spend in the thing, another suit was produced and cut into two sections for shots requiring only part of the monster, waist-up or waist-down. For screen tests of the latter, Nakajima, the stuntman, galumphed around in his heavy suspenders like someone wearing clown pants or waders, his great rubber feet crushing the rough models they'd arranged around the stage.

They chose Nakajima not only for his height and physical conditioning but also for his dogged determination. To prepare for his role, he'd taken a projector home with him and worn out Tsuburaya's print of *King Kong*, and he told anyone who would listen that he'd spent two full weeks of evenings observing bears at the Ueno Zoo.

Another unit had successfully produced a smaller-scale, hand-operated puppet of the head that could spray a stream of mist from its jaws, for close-ups of the creature's radioactive breath.

"So is your monster ready to go?" Masano asked the night before shooting was set to commence, out of the dark, when Tsuburaya had thought she was asleep.

"I think he is, yes," Tsuburaya answered, surprising even himself.

One of the first recitations that he remembered from primary school involved the five terrors, in ascending order: earthquake, storm, flood, fire, father. It surprised no one that father was judged the most dangerous. As preoccupied as fathers were, when it came to their sons they still found time for disappointment and punishment. And waiting to see that disappointment coalesce on his father's face, during those rare occasions on which Tsuburaya spent time with him: those were some of his unhappiest memories.

His academic performance was always adequate but his father was particularly unhappy about his refusal to moderate the time he devoted after school to airplane building, and in the event of a harsh report on this from his grandmother, his father gave him the option of having his most recent model-building efforts reduced to kindling or having his hand burned. Like many before him, his father believed in the deterrent effect of burning rolled wormwood fibers on the clenched fist of a misbehaving boy. Once lit, the fibers lifted off from their own convection currents after a moment or two, but even so always left behind a white scar.

Afterwards his father treated the burn himself, with a cooling paste, and talked about the lessons his own father had taught him. He always began with the maxim that with either good acts or bad, the dust thus amassed would make a mountain. He had other favorites as well. When addressing elders or the opposite sex, the mouth was the entrance to calamity. Hard work in school had its usefulness, because what seemed stupid now might prove useful later. We should love our children with a stick. And it was always better not to say than to say.

His father reminded him that in the old days a child like Tsuburaya would be made to swallow a small salamander alive as a cure for nervous weakness. One rainy morning in a park, when his father thought he'd been too peevish, he held one up to Tsuburaya's mouth and said that a childhood classmate of his had reported he could feel it moving about his stomach for some minutes afterward.

Yet Tsuburaya also remembered him taking them on the hottest days for shaved ice with grape, strawberry, or lemon syrup, the syrup never getting down as far as the red beans at the base of the paper cone. He remembered a delivery in a downpour in which they sat in their wagon watching farmers in a field in the distance, in their raincoats woven from rushes looking like so many porcupines while they squatted to rest. He remembered insect festivals in the evenings when the autumn grasses bloomed and the singing insects they'd gathered in their tiny cages were, at an agreed-upon stroke, all freed, and how they waited – himself, his grandmother, Ichiro, and his father – for that moment when the cicadas would get their bearings, puzzle out their freedom, and let loose their rejoicing in song.

For the first day of principal photography, the visual effects team was divided into its three units, one for location photography to shoot the plates for the process and composite shots, one for the lab work, and one for the miniatures. Tsuburaya called Hajime that morning to let him know that he could join the unit. Hajime was so excited that he claimed he ran all the way to the studio when the streetcar was late.

"Why didn't you take a cab?" Honda asked once he arrived. "You're sweating on our work," he added, when Hajime only grinned for an answer.

Tsuburaya told him that he had three minutes to get the film casings loaded, and the boy disappeared to cool himself off as best he could at the sinks in the washroom before returning with his hair askew and in a borrowed shirt.

It turned out that before they'd even gotten through a half a day, another stuntman, Tezuka, was needed to spell Nakajima, so exhausting was the part. The suit was stifling in the August heat even without the studio lights, but with them it was a roasting pan. Added to that were the fumes from the burning kerosene rags intended to simulate Tokyo's fires. Under the searing lights Nakajima was barely able to breathe or see, and could only spend a maximum of fifteen minutes in the suit before being too overcome to continue. Each time he stepped out of it, the supporting technicians drained the legs as if pouring water out of a boot. One measured a cup and a half of sweat from each leg.

The second half of the first day's schedule involved the destruction of the National Diet. Tezuka fainted and broke his jaw on the top of the parliament building as he fell, so they were back to Nakajima again. While awaiting Nakajima's recovery, they repaired the damage to the building.

Upon his return, everything went off in one shot. While he maneuvered his way down the row of buildings, crew members at Tsuburaya's signal heaved on the cable that ran up through a pulley in the rafters and worked the tail. When it crashed into the side of the National Diet, another technician detonated the pyrotechnics and plastic and wooden parts rained down on everyone in the studio. Honda said it looked even better through the eyepiece than they might have hoped. And they all felt at once exultation and disquiet. While the men extinguishing the fires sprayed everything down, the fastenings were undone and the top part of the creature was peeled from poor Nakajima's head and shoulders. While he was given some water it hung before him like a sack.

Tanaka came by to see the last part of the shot and reported that Mori had taken to calling what they were doing "suitmation."

"How'd the boy work out?" he asked Honda, half-teasing.

"I haven't heard any complaints," Honda told him in response. And Hajime pretended to be too absorbed in sealing the rush canisters to have heard what they said.

Masano was asleep when Tsuburaya was finally dropped off after the first day of shooting, and asleep when he left the next morning. Toward the end of the second day, an assistant informed him during a break that she'd telephoned to let him know that Hajime would be joining them for dinner that night.

His son was lugging film cans to the processing wagon while Tsuburaya read the note. "You're dining with us tonight?" he called to him.

"That's what I'm told," Hajime answered.

They rode home together. It was still bright out and the dining table was flooded with a quiet white light from the paper windows. Masano collected Imari porcelain and had set out for the occasion her most prized bowls and cups.

Seeming even more grim than usual, she asked how their

days had been. Tsuburaya told her his had gone well. Hajime smiled like a guest in someone else's home, and Akira seemed beside himself with joy at his brother's unexpected presence, though even he seemed to register the tension. For appetizers there were a number of variations on raw radishes, Hajime's favorite, including some involving three kinds of flavored salts. Masano had begun believing more and more fiercely in the purifying usefulness of salt.

There was a silence while they ate, except for Akira smacking his lips. When they finished, Masano cleared the table and served, for dessert, more radishes, pickled and sugared. She asked if they had anything to tell her.

"Do you have anything to tell your mother?" Tsuburaya asked the older boy.

Hajime seemed to give it some knit-browed thought. "It's nice to see you?" he finally offered.

She sat back with her arms folded and watched them exchange looks. "I've tried to give our son some direction; a little instruction," she finally remarked. "But you know what that's like. It's like praying into a horse's ear."

"I've taken Hajime on as my camera assistant," Tsuburaya told her.

"Yes, I thought that might be the situation," she answered, and even Akira acknowledged the extent of her anger by hunching his shoulders. "The personnel department called, needing information," she added.

He'd provided their oldest son with a job, and a good one,

Tsuburaya reminded her. That seemed cause for celebration, and not complaint.

"As you say, I have no cause for complaint," Masano told him. But something in her shoulders once she'd turned away left him so dismayed that he found he no longer had the heart to argue. They sat facing each other like mirror images of defeat.

"Thank you for this excellent meal," Hajime told her.

"Thank you for coming," Masano answered. Tsuburaya put his hand atop hers, at the table, and she let him leave it there.

But she didn't speak to him again until later that night, when he threw off his covers in the heat. She said then that as a young woman she'd felt anxious about seeming awkward when she tried to express herself. And that until she'd met him, she'd feared it had something to do with being too self-centered. And that their letters—their feelings—had helped her understand that something else was possible.

"Remember how thrilled we'd be when we saw my name in the credits?" Tsuburaya asked her.

"I read some of those letters today," she told him. In the dark he couldn't see her face. "They're such strange things. So full of connection."

"Hajime can work for Toho and remain a loving son," he told her.

"I need to sleep now," she explained, after a pause. And after another pause, she did.

He departed earlier than usual for the studio the next day, and at his driver's horn-blowing, he raised his head from his work to find his car in a great migration of bicycles ridden by delivery boys, bakery boys, and messenger boys, some of them negotiating astonishing loads: glaziers' boys balancing great panes of glass, soba boys shouldering pyramids of boxed soups, peddlers' boys with pickle barrels. All weaving along at high speed. When a toddler in a tram window reached out to touch one, the cyclist veered away down a side street.

Honda greeted him that morning with Ifukube's score, which he played for everyone on the upright piano. No surprises there. Ifukube had spent the war composing nationalist marches, and what he'd presented to Honda was a mishmash of some of his favorites. Apparently he hadn't even looked at the rushes. "Close your eyes and you're back on the Home Front," Tanaka called acidly from the hallway while Honda was playing it.

That afternoon two full sequences were filmed. After Honda approved the second, he asked if Tsuburaya had come up with anything to conceal the wires for the attacking jets. Tsuburaya showed him on the Movieola the little test he'd conducted, and Honda was stupefied and overjoyed: what had Tsuburaya done? Where had the wires gone? Tsuburaya explained that he'd hung and flown the models upside down, then had inverted the image. The wires were still there, but no one noticed them below the aircraft instead of above. Honda wanted to call some others in and make a fuss about it, but Tsuburaya reminded him that if time and budget were the main walls around the moviemaker, it was his job to help punch through them. "So we can get on to other things," Honda agreed. And Tsuburaya could imagine Masano's response, had she heard.

Early in the war they'd brought Hajime to see the rare birds and animals that had been added to the Ueno Zoo after the conquests in the south. Tsuburaya remembered the days being perpetually sunny. Hajime had also loved the rooftop pool of the Matsuzakaya department store, where shoppers were treated to mock battles between electrically controlled models of the Japanese and Allied fleets while the store's customer service manager talked about the need for consumer restraint. Plaques bearing the phrase *Honor Home* were in the windows of every house that had a father or son off at the war, and Masano had joked to her friends that only her husband's age had held him back, and that national mobilization would not be a problem if all that was asked of men was that they cast off parents, wives, or children before going off to war.

But by that point he was already working in the Special Arts Department at Toho. The ten major studios had been forced to consolidate into just three, all making mostly war films in order to promote national policy and strengthen the country's resolve. The rooftop display had given him the idea for the miniatures photography for Toho's first drama about the China war, *Navy Bomber Squadron*. And the climactic battle sequence had gone off so well that he'd then been given responsibility for the scene in which the Chinese primary school, once destroyed, turned out to have been a secret armaments depot. Those sequences had resulted in his first screen credit for visual effects, though the sight of the bombed Chinese school seemed to cripple Masano's enjoyment at the premiere.

Had they ever been closer, though? The ongoing national emergency had seemed to revive her sense of all that she still had to lose, and nearly every night her face found his in their bed once they had turned out the light. Every family was urged to start the day at the same hour with radio calisthenics, and during the first six months after Pearl Harbor there were nothing but victories to report, so the radio made for good listening. Hajime found it hilarious to watch his parents huff and sweat. More and more disappeared from public life to exist only in private, the way before the war the censors had edited out of foreign films all instances of socialism or kissing.

Accounts of each battle were concluded with a rendition of Ifukube's Naval March. But then as the war turned, announcements of this or that territory's strategic importance were reversed, and a territory's loss apparently meant nothing, whereas its capture had been wildly celebrated the year before. Hajime spent even longer hours in school undergoing mandatory vocational and military training. And Masano was further saddened at the eradication of neighborhood birds by the heavy guns of an artillery training division billeted nearby.

Tsuburaya told her one night that it was just like Japan to go to war with the nation upon whom she was most dependent for the raw materials essential to prosecuting that war. Modern warfare began in the mine and continued in the factory, feeding on coal and steel and oil, and ninety percent of the oil Japan consumed before the war was imported, nearly all of it from the United States. She seemed to find this point even more painful than he did.

They were told that Leyte was the battle that would determine the fate of the nation. Once Leyte was lost, it turned out that Luzon was the key. After Luzon, Iwo Jima. After Iwo Jima, Okinawa. "Well, apparently the mountain moves," Masano answered, a little bitterly, when he remarked to her about it. She was especially demoralized by a newspaper account of the destruction of Okinawa's capital, and the printed photo of their narrow and hushed streets from all those years ago shelled into rubble.

By then there were no pleasures. Food was miserable, lovemaking was impossible, there was no time even for reading, and they constantly feared that even at his age Hajime would be called up. Dinners were rice bran, fried in a pan, which looked like custard but made Hajime cry when he ate it. Movie production had come to a halt due to a lack of nitrate for film stock. Workers at Toho were serving as labor volunteers in the countryside, helping farmers and returning each night with a few sweet potatoes for their work.

And then came the raids. Hajime demanded to be taken to a public exhibition of a B-29 in Hibiya Park, where the bomber had been reconstructed from the parts of various downed aircraft and was displayed alongside one of Japan's latest interceptors. The fighter looked like a peanut beside a dinner plate. Such was the Americans' nonchalance by that point that they dropped leaflets the day before detailing where and when they would strike. Aloft, these leaflets resembled a small, fleecy cloud, but as they fluttered down they dispersed over the city.

The fire raid on March 9th centered on the area hit by the 1923 earthquake, the trauma that had separated him forever from his father. The one on the 10th extended the destruction. The next morning they returned to acres of ruin where their homes had been. Block after block was burned flat, with lonely telephone poles erect at odd angles like grave markers, leaving only ash and brick and the occasional low shell of a concrete building. Where the desolation wasn't complete, the neighborhood associations were still holding air defense drills and doing their best to resettle those bombed out of their homes.

The only topic of conversation by then was food, or the failure of the rationing system. Everyone spent their days foraging. They were told to collect acorns for flour because they had the same nutritive value as rice. They ate weeds and boiled licorice greens and bracken ferns. And then they heard that as the result of an attack by a very small number of B-29's, the city of Hiroshima had been considerably damaged. And that the Emperor would be addressing the nation by radio for the first time in history.

When Tsuburaya mentioned by way of offering encouragement that they'd completed the first month of shooting, Masano said in response, "You take as much time as you need to. Whatever your lack of interest, our routine is going to continue as it has."

He was taken aback. She'd caught him struggling into his rain shell and preoccupied with the problem of the high tension wires the monster was to destroy on his way into Tokyo. She was at their kitchen table working on a gourd that was supposed to afford the sparrows some protection from rats. The gourd would hang from a nail under the eave outside their front door.

This wasn't how things would always be, he assured her. Soon the shooting and even post-production would be over.

"I'll continue to maintain your household and raise your child, whatever happens between us," she told him.

"What does that mean: 'whatever happens between us'?"

he asked. He was shaken, the notion of yet more separation like a fear of the dark.

"Akira's very proud of you," she answered. "And his brother. Do you know what he said to me before he left for school? He said he understood why neither of you liked him."

"Do I need to stay home?" Tsuburaya asked her, and set down his work satchel. "Do we need to talk about this now?"

"He's nine years old and he sounded like me," she said.

He unbuckled his rain shell in contrition, pained at her attempt to keep her composure. "I'll talk to him this evening," he told her. "Hajime will talk to him as well."

"It's one thing if it's just myself," she said. "But I can't watch this happen to him, too."

"I'll go see him now," he said. He had his driver wait outside Akira's school, but the boy's classroom was empty when he finally found it. The instructor in an adjacent room said he thought the class might have gone off on a nature walk.

When Tsuburaya was twenty-two, his father took the train to Tokyo for business and left his grandmother and Ichiro in charge of the store. The idea seemed to be that he might partner up with a larger distribution chain. But he might also have been trying to exert some influence on his son.

Tsuburaya had by that point given up his dreams of aviation, and after serving in the Imperial infantry had returned to the store, uncertain of his future. Before his call-up, a chance encounter had led to his training as a cameraman for Edamasa, the famous director, whom he'd worked for until his conscription notice had arrived. Back at home, he stocked shelves and took inventory. His father claimed his son's choices were his own, but his grandmother hectored him to give up dreaming about movies and airplanes and to give some thought to his family and especially his father and uncle, who shouldered the burden of the family business alone.

But when he heard from Edamasa again, the pull was too strong, and when he was sent out to buy rice one morning, he left a note stating he wouldn't return until he'd succeeded in the motion picture business or died trying. When he telephoned from Tokyo a week later to let them know he was safe and settled into a place where they could reach him, Ichiro came to the phone but his father and grandmother did not. Ichiro said his mother still hadn't recovered from the effrontery of the note.

So he was surprised to receive his father's invitation to lunch. They arranged it for the day of his father's arrival, but that morning the truck had broken down on some location shooting for which Tsuburaya had volunteered in the hills and he found himself stranded out of town.

The day his truck broke down and his father arrived at the capital was September 1st, 1923, and a few minutes before noon his father was still expecting him for lunch when the Great Kanto Earthquake brought the Imperial Hotel's chandelier down onto the table before him. He said he'd just lifted his water glass away from his place setting when it was as if a giant had stamped it flat.

He stood up with his pant leg open at the knee like a haversack. Something in the shattered and telescoping table had lashed open his lower thigh.

The moment before, he'd been peering over at the lunch room's little indoor pond, where dull carp drowsed in the tepid water. Then there was a rumbling and the first shock, a vertical jolt. At the second jolt, the chandelier came down, and the floor began to pitch and rock so that the heavy parquet snapped and ricocheted like fireworks, and after he'd stood he was unable to run and got thrown onto his side. From there he saw the office concern across the street collapse into a dust cloud so intense that it was as if the hotel windows had been permanently chalked with yellow.

Out on a side street, he managed to tie his tattered pant leg around his thigh, casting around for his son, and with every jolt the hotel and an adjacent bank flexed like buggy whips and cracks appeared along their walls, from which window casings and marble avalanched into the street. He said that with each shock it was as if the earth had been pulled out from under him. Where was Eiji? Where was his son? He ran, searching, as the concussions changed to undulations. And then it appeared to be over, though every few minutes the aftershocks were sufficient to knock to him to his knees.

He found himself in a little park, panting. Sparrows under a stand of orange trees seemed somehow to have been grounded, hopping about, for all the freneticism of their wings achieving only a few feet of altitude before fluttering back into the dirt. He·was weeping, he realized, in fear for his son. Should he go back? All avenues in that direction had been blocked by massive slides of debris.

All of this he'd related to Ichiro the last time Tsuburaya saw him. Only the oval of his face had been spared the salve and the bandages. Tsuburaya had wondered if the doctors had applied the same cooling paste his father had used on his burns. He said hello to his father, who then directed him and his grandmother to wait outside the ward. His grandmother went off to berate the overworked medical teams from the Relief Bureau, but he held his ear to the open door.

"Keep him away from me," his father said, and Tsuburaya couldn't fully register what he'd just heard. His father went on to tell his uncle that within a minute the city had been cut off from everything, the water and gas mains ruptured, the telegraph and telephone wires down. The trolley rails where he crossed them had sprung upward after snapping. He'd called for Eiji and in response heard cries in all directions. And then he noticed the rice cracker shop already on fire, the smoke rising into the still, hot air. There seemed to be no one present, no one making an effort to put out the flames.

Later Tsuburaya thought that he'd probably heard more of his father's voice that day than he had for the previous five years. He was crying for his father's pain and because of his banishment from the room. Every so often Ichiro asked if the pain was very bad and never received an answer. When his grandmother returned, she whispered something and tried to pull Tsuburaya away from the door, but he tore his elbow away with such ferocity that she never tried again. You should go back into that room, he told himself. Instead he stood where he was and listened.

Everything had been destroyed and the gas mains shattered just as lunch fires were being lit in hibachis and stoves all over Tokyo, in hotels and lunch counters and apartments and factory work stations from Ota to Arakawa. All of those braziers scattered their coals onto tatami mats on crooked old streets and alleys just wide enough to provide sufficient drafts. His father saw firemen—their water mains now dry—trying to use nearby moats and canals. He said those not trying to pull the trapped from the rubble did their best to put out the fires, but there were too many of them, and almost no water. Then the wind picked up.

Because there was no single point of origin, neither was there a single advancing front of fire, and no one knew where to go or what was safe. Everyone who could headed to the river, and along its banks the mobs were increasingly herded toward the bridges, where they were crushed or tipped over the side until the bridges themselves caught fire. His father struggled toward anyone who resembled his son until he was knocked into the water by a handcart, and there he stayed alive by keeping submerged until oil from ruptured storage tanks ignited upstream, the fire cascading at him along the surface. He scrambled out just ahead of its arrival.

Beside the Yasuda Gardens he pitched himself into a broad, bare lot that had been the site of the Army Clothing Depot, where uniforms were stored for shipment. Its size and location along the river promised more safety – across its twelve acres there was very little to burn – and thousands poured into it all through the afternoon, as everywhere else became more and more of a conflagration. They came singly and in groups, some pulling carts piled with outlandish goods, and found places for themselves. Patients from nearby hospitals were carried in on stretchers. Everyone was polite, settling down shoulder to shoulder to wait. They watched the fires surrounding them burn. The crush was so pronounced that he gave up the notion of hunting the crowd for his son.

Someone behind him complained that he'd forgotten his chess set. The bitter taste of smoke in the air intensified. He wished he'd had some lunch.

And then, across the river, starbursts of sparks and flame seemed to be climbing the columns of smoke high into the clouds. He asked the man beside him for the time, and the man told him it was a little after four. The wind was intensifying, and from the west they could hear the sound of a huge airplane flying low across the river. Was it a rescue mission? It was flying towards them, but in that direction the sky was enveloped in black. And then he saw it wasn't the sky but a column so wide it seemed to cover the horizon, and that it was spinning and shot through with fire. Debris crossed its face and reappeared again. By then they could hear nothing else.

It seemed to detonate everything on the other side of the river before it came across. It swept away the barges. It blew apart the School of Industry. It drew river water forty feet up into the funnel before it sheared off as steam. By the time it hit the Clothing Depot it sounded like gargantuan waterfalls crashing together.

Two policemen agape on a refugee's cart were blown away. Tsuburaya's father was knocked down and blasted along the ground until his hand caught onto something. A teenaged girl on fire flew by over his head. Human beings all around him were sucked into the air like sparks. He shut his eyes against the wind and heat. A tree was wrenched from the ground, roots and all, before him, and he crawled into the loose earth and was able to breathe. Some ruptured water mains there had created a bog, and he tunneled into the mud.

When he revived, the backs of his hands had been burned to the bone. Everyone was gone. The skin atop his head was gone. His ears were gone. Something beside him he couldn't recognize was still squirming.

At their store that evening, two hundred and twenty kilometers away, Tsuburaya's grandmother reported that the columns of smoke and cloud carried upward by the convection currents made everyone wonder if a new volcano had been born. An intense red glow spread across the southern horizon.

His father said he remembered only fitful things afterward. Someone carried him somewhere eventually. An Army cart in one of the burned-out areas stopped to pass out cupfuls of water to refugees. A riderless horse stood in the road too badly burned to move. Bodies looked like black rucksacks except for the occasional raised leg or hand. He remembered a shirt like his son's under a cascade of lumber. A functioning well with a long queue beside it. He died soon after he mentioned the well, describing the water he so enjoyed from it.

In the years following his father's death, Tsuburaya talked to historians and scientists and survivors. The historians informed him that over four thousand acres of Tokyo had burned, ten times the Great Fire of London's, and that a hundred thousand people had perished, a hundred times the number consumed in the Americans' San Francisco fire. The scientists informed him that the updraft that produced the columns his grandmother witnessed had caused a gigantic vacuum near the ground and the surrounding air had swept in to fill it before being drawn upwards itself, resulting in a furnace four thousand acres wide and an updraft that generated tornadoes as it pulled the fire up into it: fire tornadoes. And the survivors told him stories like the ones his father had related. Though of course once Masano and Tsuburaya had endured the fire raids at the end of the war, he no longer needed to turn to others for that sort of understanding. "Smoke Tsuburaya," she'd said to herself one night as they'd hurried down the steps to a shelter. He'd had less trouble than others negotiating a safe route through the fires, since he knew from his father's experience which way to go.

"Do you think he knew I was listening?" he'd asked his uncle on the morning his family had returned home from his father's deathbed. He'd shamed himself by weeping so much on the train that his grandmother had finally taken a seat opposite him.

"I don't think he gave it any thought," Ichiro answered.

At the sound bay, everyone was very excited about the roar Ifukube had come up with. Tsuburaya had charged him with the task of creating for the monster's cry something melancholy and ear-splitting—"Try producing *that* combination," Ifukube had complained when given the instructions—and he'd spent two weeks sorting through recordings of wild animals before he'd finally given up and settled on drawing a heavy work glove across the strings of a contrabass and manipulating the sound in an echo chamber. The result was hair-raising. The entire production team was beside itself with happiness. He had also overlaid a recording of a taiko drum with an electronically altered mine detonation to produce the monster's footfalls.

•

Halfway through the shooting Honda told Tsuburaya that he was using many more close-ups of the monster's face than he'd thought he would, because the monster's dilemma was becoming more real to him. Man had created war and the Bomb and now nature was going to exact its revenge, with tormented Gojira its way of making radiation visible. That's why he'd insisted that the monster's skin be thick and furrowed like the keloid scars of the atomic survivors.

Tanaka was uneasy, in fact, with how often the movie referenced the war. And he worried that the long shots of the burned-out city would recall for everyone the newspaper images of Hiroshima and Nagasaki.

In the rushes of the final scenes, Honda noted how sad Gojira looked when he turned from the camera.

"That's the way I made the mask," Tsuburaya reminded him.

"No," Honda said. "The face itself is changing through the context of what we've seen him go through. By the time the movie ends he's like a hero whose departure we regret. The paradox of fearsomeness and longing is what the whole thing's about."

"I wouldn't know about that," Tsuburaya told him.

"It's like part of *us* leaving," Honda said. "That's what makes it so hard. The monster the child knows best is the monster he feels himself to be." After Tsuburaya didn't respond, he added, "That's why I love those shots of the city after the monster's gone. All that emptiness, like a no-man's land in which eloquence and silence are joined. If you don't have both, the dread evaporates."

That was true, Tsuburaya conceded. He volunteered that he was particularly proud of the shots of the harbor at night before the creature's eruption from the sea: all along the waterfront, silence. Silence like thunder.

Akira was turned to the wall in his sleep when Tsuburaya got home. One foot hung over the pallet, exposing an impossibly thin ankle. He left for the boy a little maquette that the team had used to model Gojira's head, standing it on the floor next to his mat.

Masano had apparently taken to mounting amulets throughout the house where their influence was desired, against pestilence at the doorway or against storms on the ceiling. The house was dark and still. Tsuburaya went through some old production notes at his desk. Atop one of the shot lists he found some gingko leaves and a note from Akira. His instructor at school had told him they kept the bookworms away.

"I'm a bad father," Tsuburaya told Honda before his unit got started the next morning. His friend seemed unfazed by the news, so he added, "A bad husband, too."

"Supposedly the cat forgets in three days the kindnesses of three years," Honda answered.

They shot the scene of the creature crashing through the rail yards at Shinagawa. The suit's rubber feet were continually torn up by even the thinnest steel of the model rails, and shot after shot after shot proved unsatisfactory. Some of their work was as repetitive as a carpenter's hammering. But the house still had to be built.

Tsuburaya repaired the feet himself with cotton swabs and a glue pot and a fine brush while Nakajima drank tea and enjoyed the break. Handcraftsmanship justified itself as an expression of intimacy with the world. Honda made jokes about the number of people standing around on salary, but Tsuburaya reminded him that the potter accepted long hours at the kiln with his body and soul.

"That's good to know," Honda responded. "But in the meantime, nobody gets to eat."

Mori mounted a publicity blitz four full weeks before the release, including an eleven-installment radio serial, and by the premiere their monster's face glowered down from every bus and tramway stop, and a nearly full-sized Gojira balloon swayed and bowed in the wind over an automobile dealership in the Ginza district.

It worked: *Gojira* recorded the best opening-day ticket sales in Tokyo's history and had a better first week than Ku-

46

rosawa's *Seven Samurai*. "It's like a dream!" Akira shrieked at the showing his family attended, and Masano watched the destruction in respectful silence. Some of the older audience members left the theater in tears.

Mori had already begun to arrange the sequel. Since *Gojira* ended with the scientist's warning that if the world continued with nuclear weapons there would someday appear another such monster, the sequel would involve two: Gojira and his bitter enemy, yet to be designed. One possibility for the latter appeared to Tsuburaya in a dream the night after the premiere, a gigantic tussock moth rendered with enough scientific accuracy that its face and mouth parts were horrific. In the dream it was obsessed with two magical little girls. Tsuburaya even glimpsed the teaser line: *The Mightiest Monster in All Creation—Ravishing a Universe for Love.*

American investors had already won the auction for *Gojira*'s international rights and decided to add new footage involving an American reporter trapped in Tokyo during the rampage, in order to give Western audiences someone for whom to care. They announced they were also going to tone down the nuclear references. They retitled it *Godzilla*, and added the subtitle *King of the Monsters*.

A month after the premiere, Tsuburaya walked home alone late one December night, bundled against the cold. In the fishmonger's shop the dried bonito looked like whetstones

47

in the window. He stopped at a sushi stall for some boiled rice with vinegar.

The boy who served him had a bamboo crest motif on his coat and he asked why Tsuburaya was smiling. Tsuburaya nearly told him that in all of his work he'd always been looking for the patterns that were an object's essence, and that on the boy's coat the bamboo was an emblem of the living bamboo there inside it. The best patterns became the nation's communal property, like that bamboo or England's lion. Or his monster.

The boy suddenly asked why he was weeping. He said he was weeping for all that he'd been granted, and for everything he'd thrown away, then thanked the boy for his concern.

In his toast at the dinner following the premiere, Honda had noted that Tsuburaya's success was centered around his talent for developing a team and uncaging each member's skills. He joked that Tsuburaya led by example and cajoling and intimidation, that for him nothing was ever perfect and no one was ever finished, and he got a laugh by concluding that a day with Tsuburaya was like four with Kurosawa, in the way that it consigned someone ever more irrevocably to misery.

For Tsuburaya on nights like that December night, a long walk meant an even later arrival. In his father's childhood, after sunset, villages were dark and quiet and cold. A gong might call worshippers to the candlelit temple. A dog might bark. Otherwise what one saw and heard was up to the moonlight and wind.

Masano hadn't spoken to him about the movie, though she had told Hajime that by the end she'd been moved by how profoundly it had affected the other patrons her age. That December night, the moment Tsuburaya finally arrived at home, Hajime announced he was leaving to work on a picture in Malaysia. Masano stopped serving from her platter and looked at her husband as though all had been fine before he'd come in. "There he is with his warm smile," she finally said to Hajime. "Orchestrating his catastrophes."

"This wasn't his idea; it was mine," Hajime answered.

Akira stood up from the table and ran from the room, distraught at his brother's announcement.

"We'll be sorry to see you go," Tsuburaya told his son.

"The only thing you're sorry about is a production delay," Masano told him, and Tsuburaya remembered that crows supposedly couldn't feel the sun's heat because they'd already been scorched black.

She went off to see to Akira, and Hajime finished his meal in silence. Tsuburaya retired to his study and noted that the nowhere in which he chose to dwell was the abode of perfect focus. He was like the blind old teacher who never knew to stop lecturing when the breeze blew out the light.

He told Hajime this story at the station the next day while they waited for the train. That he had difficulty keeping his son's attention made him as sad as the departure. Hajime finally said that he'd rarely heard Tsuburaya talk so much before. The train pulled in, and they were silent while the arriving passengers streamed off. They might both have been imagining Akira, back in his room alone.

"Your brother's going to be very sad to see you go," Tsuburaya finally said.

This seemed to irk Hajime. "When did I become the villain?" he asked.

"No one's calling you a villain," Tsuburaya told him.

Hajime handed his bag up to the porter. "You know who you've always reminded me of?" he asked. "Prince Konoye. The two of you, actually." Then he climbed the steps to the car.

Tsuburaya was too surprised to respond. He did manage to ask Hajime if he had enough money, but the porter's departure call distracted them both and the train pulled out. Once it gathered some momentum Hajime waved, once, before his car passed out of sight around the curve with surprising speed.

Tsuburaya was left on the platform, where he remained after the other well-wishers had left. The wind swept a seed pod of some sort onto his foot.

Konoye had been Prime Minister before the attack on Pearl Harbor. He'd always understood what war with America would mean but with each new step towards destruction had lacked the will to insist that the nation do what was right. The joke about him had been that he was so perpetually unsure of his intentions he sometimes got lost en route to the toilet.

Tsuburaya and Masano had talked about Konoye more than once, especially after his death. She'd been very upset about it, in fact. He had poisoned himself before his arrest by the Americans, leaving behind in his room only his family seal and a book, the newspapers had reported. In the book, written by the Englishman Oscar Wilde, Konoye had underlined a single passage, as if he'd hoped to make his amends in pencil: *Nobody great or small can be ruined except by his own hand, and terrible as was what the world did to me, even more terrible still was what I did to myself.*

JIM SHEPARD is the author of numerous novels and short stories, including the collections *Like You'd Understand, Anyway*; *Love and Hydrogen*; and *Batting Against Castro*, as well as the novels *Project X* and *Nosferatu*. He has won the Story Prize and been nominated for the National Book Award. He lives in Massachusetts and teaches at Williams College.